First paperback edition 1994
Reprinted 1995

First published 1985 in hardback by A & C Black (Publishers) Ltd
35 Bedford Row, London WC1R 4JH
ISBN 0–7136–4111–8

A CIP catalogue record for this book is available from the British Library.

Acknowledgements
The author and publishers would like to thank Mr Dang Phuoc Tri, and the
Society for Anglo-Chinese Understanding for their help and advice, the staff and
pupils of Parsloes Primary and, most of all, Dat and the Tran family.

Filmset by August Filmsetting, Haydock, St Helens
Printed in Hong Kong by Imago

New Baby

Judith Baskerville
Photographs by Jenny Matthews

A & C Black · London

It's today!
It's Iqbal's birthday.
He's seven years old so
he's having a party with
his friends.

The party is to celebrate
that very special day
when Iqbal was born –
his 'birth-day'.

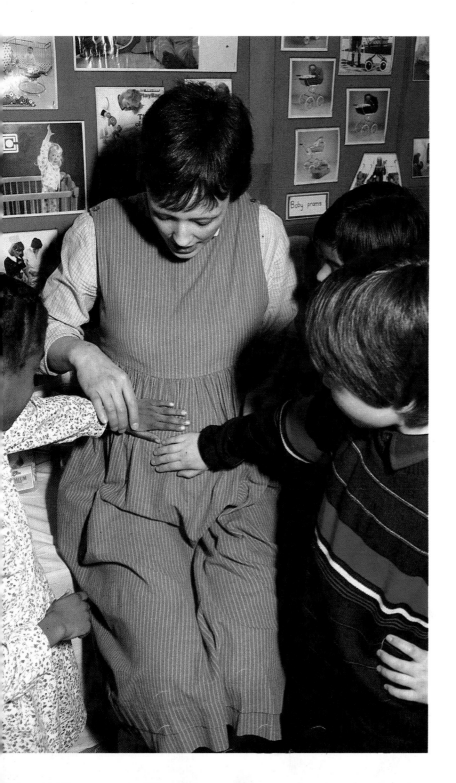

Iqbal's teacher has a friend called Judith. She is pregnant and soon she is going to have her baby.

No-one knows when the baby's birthday will be. No-one even knows whether the baby will be a boy or a girl.

3

Judith has been pregnant all through summer, autumn and winter. A baby grows inside its mother for about nine months. Then it is ready to be born.

How big do you think you were when you first started to grow? Iqbal's class is making a display to show you.

After one month you were smaller than a 'hundreds and thousands'. After two months you were about the size of a two-pence piece. After three months you were as long as a fish-finger.

Look to see how long you were after four months, five months and six months . . .

. . . after seven months and eight months.

How long were you when you were born?

(Don't forget that these pictures only show the *length* of the baby, and a baby is always curled up inside its mother.)

At home, Judith's family is busy getting ready for the baby. Neil is the baby's father. Alex and Nicola will soon have a new sister or brother. It's exciting for everyone.

Judith and Neil fetch Nicola's old pram from the attic. Can you see where the baby will sleep?

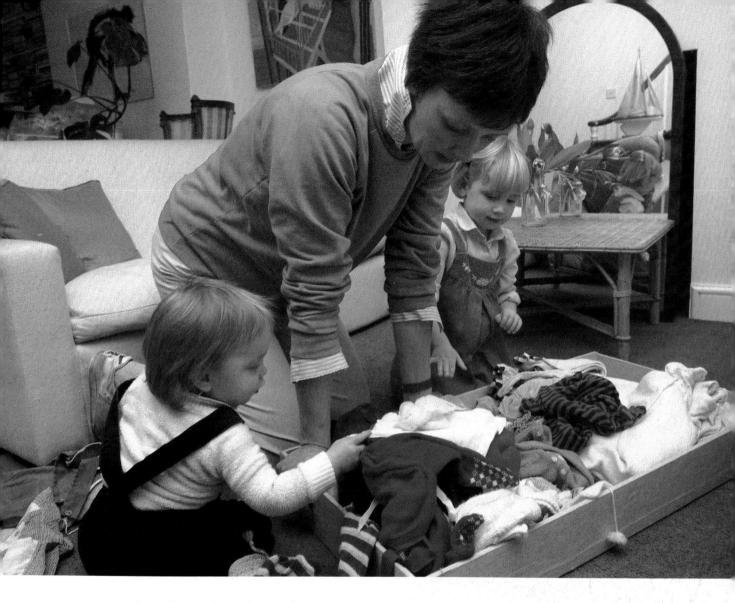

Look at the size of the baby's clothes. Everything needs to be washed and then put away, ready for when the baby arrives.

Everyone helps. Some friends have lent Judith their old baby clothes and Granny is knitting a cardigan.

The children from school help too. They are going shopping with Judith. They need to buy a 'baby-gro' and some vests for the baby.

When you were a baby, what did you wear?

It's very difficult to remember what it was like being a baby. But you could find some old photographs to see what you looked like.

Lee and Natasha made books about themselves.
How have they changed since they were babies?

Lee and his mum had an argument about an old
photograph. His mum said that the photograph
was of Lee's brother. Lee couldn't believe it.
The photograph looked just like him.

Lee

Natasha as a baby with her mum.

Babies have so much to learn. They even have to learn that their hands are part of their own bodies. Have you ever seen a baby playing with its hands – staring at them, clenching them and waving them about?

To help babies learn we give them toys to play with.
Natasha is making a teddy bear for Judith's baby.
John is making a bright woolly ball.

The toys are soft and cuddly so they can't hurt the baby.

The baby has finally arrived!
It's a girl.
Everyone is happy and excited.
Now it's time to celebrate.

Judith's friends and relatives come to see her in hospital. Some of the children from school come too. They all bring cards and flowers.

Danny helps to look after the baby.

A few days later Judith and the baby go home.

Alex and Nicola meet their new sister for the first time. It's exciting but also a bit strange. It's going to take a while to get used to being a family of five.

Alex is very proud. All she wants to do is hold the baby.

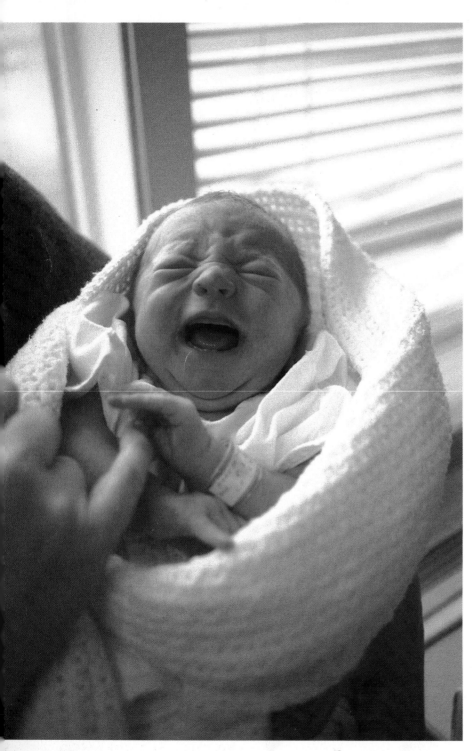

Now we know when the baby's 'birth-day' is. She was born on the eighth of February.

We know that the baby is a girl, too. But what will Judith and Neil decide to call her?

How did your parents choose your name? You might be named after a relative or a friend of your family.

Iqbal's name has a special meaning.
It means 'prosperity'.
That's success, good health and happiness all in one word. What a lovely meaning for a name.

Judith and Neil decide to call their baby Jenny, just because they like the name. It's short for Jennifer. Is your name short for something?

BIRTHS

BASKERVILLE. – On February 8th, to Judith (nee Pickles) and Neil, a third daughter (Jennifer Kim) – and sister for Alex and Nicola.

Judith and Neil put an announcement in the newspaper. It tells everyone that the eighth of February will always be a very special day for the family.

There are lots of different ways to celebrate a baby's birth. Some families have religious celebrations.

Danny's family is Christian. When Danny was a few weeks old his family took him to church. Danny was given his name and christened by the vicar. Then prayers were said for Danny and his family.

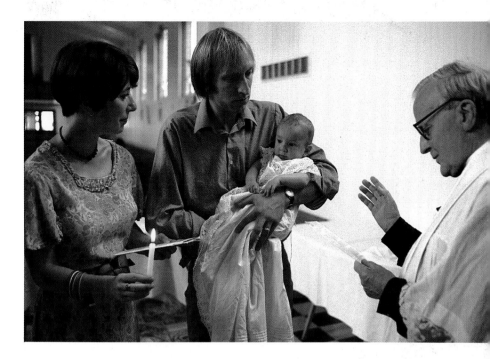

Muslim families, like Iqbal's, might ask their Imam to come and see the new baby. The Imam whispers the special call to prayer in the baby's ear. Later, the baby is given a name.

When you were born, how did your family celebrate?

At school the children are going to have a birthday party for Jenny.

Iqbal, Neamo and Joseph are making a chocolate birthday cake. But how many candles should they put on the cake?

Jenny isn't even one year old, so Sonya makes a special 0 candle. Can you see it on the cake?

Jenny is too young to understand that it's her birthday party. She spends most of the time fast asleep. But Judith is going to keep all the cards and presents. Jenny can play with them later on.

Jenny is so very small. It's funny to think that one day she will be a grown-up person.

She might have children of her own. Then Judith and Neil would be grandparents. Their family could keep growing bigger and bigger.

There's a special way of showing how families grow.
It's called a family tree.
This is Jenny's family tree.

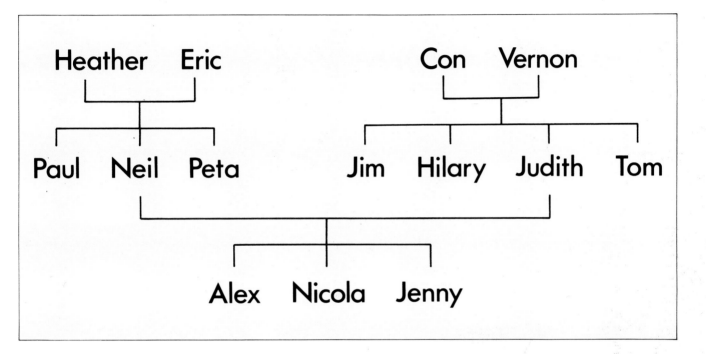

You can make your own family tree. As your family grows, you can add new people to the tree.

One day, you may be able to show it to your children.

Jenny is learning new things every day. Soon she'll be able to do all the things that you enjoy.

What are the best things that have ever happened to you? Sometimes it's hard to decide. But whatever they are, wouldn't you like to think that Jenny could enjoy them too?

Things to do

There are lots of things in this book that you can try for yourself, such as making a family tree or a book of baby photographs. Here are some more things which you can do.

1. Ask your mum and dad what happened when you were born. Try to find out about the people who helped with the birth, such as doctors, midwives or nurses.

When you were born, did your family have a religious celebration? What happened? Who helped with the celebrations – a Vicar, a Priest, a Rabbi an Imam, a Pundit, or someone else? Compare stories with your friends.

2. Jenny is short for Jennifer. Have you ever heard stories about King Arthur and the Knights of the Round Table? Arthur's wife was called Guenevere. Over the years the name Guenevere has changed to Jennifer. If you say the two names out loud you can hear how alike they sound. Try to find out if your name has changed in this way, or if your name has a special meaning.

3. Try changing your 'home corner' into a 'new baby corner'. What will you need?

4. Find out more about babies' toys. You may be able to visit a museum to see some old-fashioned toys.

5. Try making some babies' toys. You can also look for rhymes and songs which babies might enjoy, or you can make up some songs and rhymes of your own.

6. Ask your teacher or an older member of your family if they have any photographs of themselves as babies. Look at the photographs to see how people have changed. Look at the clothes which they wore. How are they different from babies' clothes today?

Books for you to read
Kate's Party, *by J. Solomon* (Hamish Hamilton)
How you Began, *by H. Spiers* (Dent)
Momoko's Birthday, *by C. Iwasaki* (Bodley Head)
The Baby's Catalogue, *by J. and A. Ahlberg* (Kestrel)
A Name for Manjit's Sister (*The English Language Centre, Markhouse School, London E17*)

Books for your parents or teacher
Tracing your Family Tree, *by S. Colwell* (Faber)
Milestones – Rites of Passage in Multifaith Communities, *by C. Collinson & C. Miller* (Edward Arnold)
Oxford Dictionary of English Christian Names, *Withycombe* (Oxford University Press)
Muslim Names and their Meanings, *by Z. Malik* (Asran Study Centre)
Naming Patterns (Minority Group Support Service, Coventry Education Authority)